YETI AND THE BIRD

written and illustrated by

Nadia Shireen

atheneum

Atheneum Books for Young Readers

New York · London · Toronto · Sydney · New Delhi

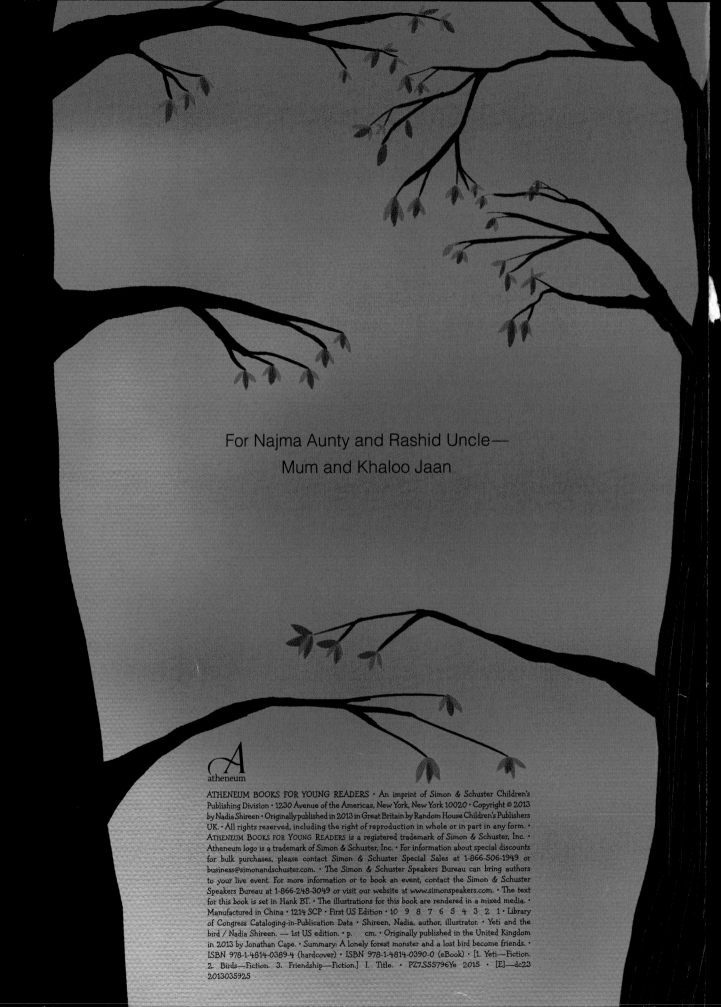

For Najma Aunty and Rashid Uncle—
Mum and Khaloo Jaan

ATHENEUM BOOKS FOR YOUNG READERS · An imprint of Simon & Schuster Children's
Publishing Division · 1230 Avenue of the Americas, New York, New York 10020 · Copyright © 2013
by Nadia Shireen · Originally published in 2013 in Great Britain by Random House Children's Publishers
UK. · All rights reserved, including the right of reproduction in whole or in part in any form. ·
ATHENEUM BOOKS FOR YOUNG READERS is a registered trademark of Simon & Schuster, Inc. ·
Atheneum logo is a trademark of Simon & Schuster, Inc. · For information about special discounts
for bulk purchases, please contact Simon & Schuster Special Sales at 1-866-506-1949 or
business@simonandschuster.com. · The Simon & Schuster Speakers Bureau can bring authors
to your live event. For more information or to book an event, contact the Simon & Schuster
Speakers Bureau at 1-866-248-3049 or visit our website at www.simonspeakers.com. · The text
for this book is set in Hank BT. · The illustrations for this book are rendered in a mixed media. ·
Manufactured in China · 1214 SCP · First US Edition · 10 9 8 7 6 5 4 3 2 1 · Library
of Congress Cataloging-in-Publication Data · Shireen, Nadia, author, illustrator. · Yeti and the
bird / Nadia Shireen. — 1st US edition. · p.   cm. · Originally published in the United Kingdom
in 2013 by Jonathan Cape. · Summary: A lonely forest monster and a lost bird become friends. ·
ISBN 978-1-4814-0389-4 (hardcover) · ISBN 978-1-4814-0390-0 (eBook) · [1. Yeti—Fiction.
2. Birds—Fiction. 3. Friendship—Fiction.] I. Title. · PZ7.S55796Ye 2015 · [E]—dc23
2013035925

Deep in the forest
there lived a yeti.

He was the

BIGGEST,
hairiest,
SCARIEST

beast anyone

had ever seen.

So everyone
left him alone.

But Yeti was lonely.

Then one day . . .

THUNK!

Something

landed

on his head.

It was a bird.

And this little bird
didn't seem scared
of Yeti at all.

Sqwalka-
Sqwalka-
Sqwalka!

Not one BIT.

Instead,
the bird told
Yeti all about
her journey.

She seemed to think she
had landed on a hot,
tropical island
for the winter.

"Grooo?" said Yeti.

And sure enough, when the bird
looked for sunshine and palm trees,
there weren't any. . . . She was lost.

The bird stopped
bouncing and chirping.

PAT PAT PAT

Yeti wasn't sure what to do
with the sad little thing.

After a while, he
decided to pick up
the bird and take
her home.

The next day, the forest
woke to a peculiar sight.

Yeti and the bird were playing!

And Yeti was laughing with a hearty roar nobody had heard before.

Every evening, the friends
sang sweet, sad songs together,
which soothed the forest to sleep.

Yeti wished the bird could stay forever.
But it was getting colder, and he knew
that soon his small friend
would need to fly away.

So Yeti carefully examined
the bird's map and found out where she
needed to go.

Then he made sure she was
packed and ready for the
long journey ahead.

Yeti sighed. Without the bird,
he was even lonelier than before.

Until . . .

some new friends
came out to play.

THUD!

Deep in the forest
there lives a yeti . . .
with all his new friends.

And every now and then,
an old friend pops by to say hello.